DETROIT PUBLIC LIBRARY
3 5674 04881128 6

P9-EMH-107

Kitchen Dance

by Maurie J. Manning

CLARION BOOKS • NEW YORK

For my daughter, Dani

Clarion Books
a Houghton Mifflin Company imprint
215 Park Avenue South, New York, NY 10003

The illustrations were executed in digital watercolor,
Conté crayon, and chalk.
The text was set in 24-point Coop Forged.

www.clarionbooks.com

Manufactured in China

Library of Congress Cataloging-in-Publication Data

Manning, Maurie.
Kitchen dance / by Maurie J. Manning.
p. cm.
Summary: Two sleepy children sneak out of their beds to watch as their parents,
who love each other very much, break into a dance while washing the dishes.
ISBN 978-0-618-99110-5
[1. Bedtime—Fiction. 2. Family life—Fiction. 3. Hispanic Americans—Fiction.] I. Title.

PZ7.M315615Ki 2008
[E]—dc22
2007036838

C&C 10 9 8 7 6 5 4 3 2 1

Splash!

Clunk!

Clang!

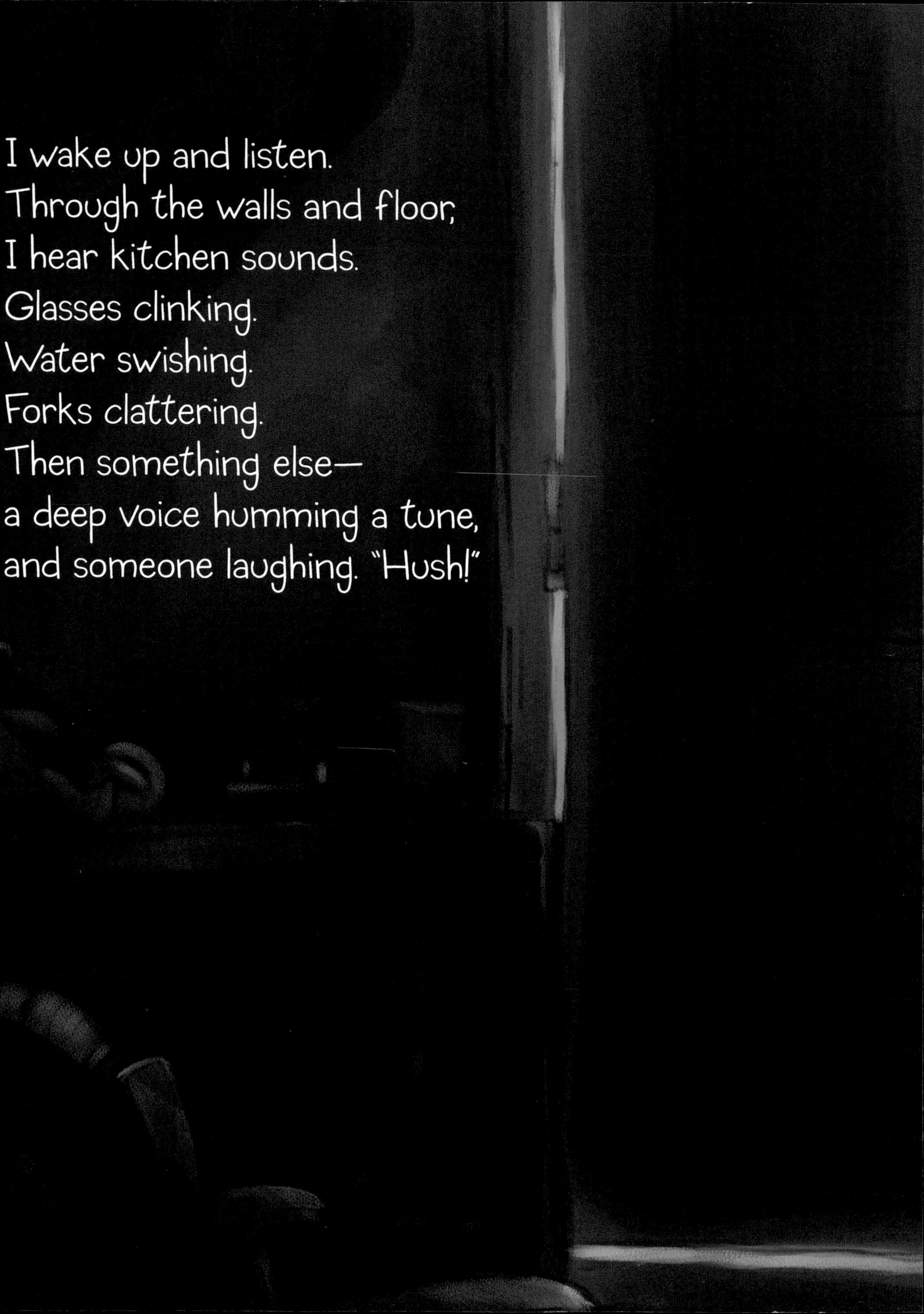

I wake up and listen.
Through the walls and floor,
I hear kitchen sounds.
Glasses clinking.
Water swishing.
Forks clattering.
Then something else—
a deep voice humming a tune,
and someone laughing. "Hush!"

I slip out of my blankets and climb up
to where Tito sleeps.

"¡Oye! Do you hear?"

Scrape

Hmm

Clang

Tito listens. He rubs the sleep from his eyes, and we climb down the ladder.

We tiptoe down the stairs,
following the sounds.

Hmm

Clunk

Shh! We creep closer
and crack open the door.

A bright skirt flashes by! Four feet fly!

My father sings a Spanish song into a wooden spoon.

"¡Cómo te quiero! Oh, how I love you. Umm, hmm."

Side by side with stacked plates they glide.
My father twirls my mother by one hand.
Laughing, she spins into his arms,
then out again, like a yo-yo on a string.

A bump of her soft hips,
and cabinet doors shut—

bang!

One, two—pots clang into their spots in the cupboard. A third gets dried with the swipe of a cotton cloth.

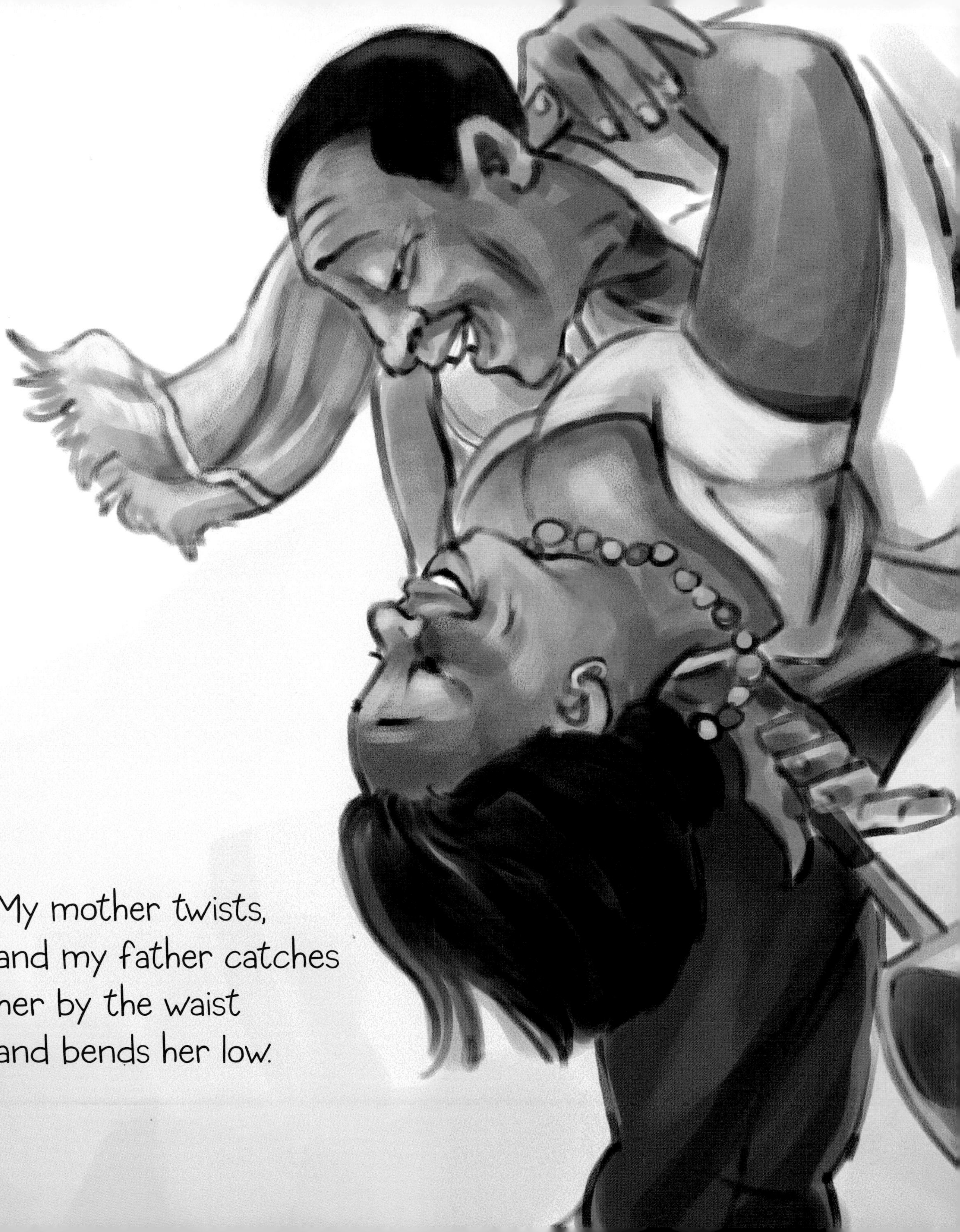

My mother twists,
and my father catches
her by the waist
and bends her low.

There is silence
for a moment.
Then . . .

. . . around the kitchen they sweep,
feet tapping, water dripping, sponge wiping,
towel snapping.

My mother's voice joins my father's,
hers high and his low. Together they tango
across the room with the leftover tamales.

Suddenly, Mama spies our peeking faces.

Tito and I squeal and turn to run, but Papa swings the door wide and catches us. "¡Hola!"

Mama holds out her hand, and I run to her.
Now eight feet fly! Papa and Tito spin by.
Mama lifts me up and swings me high.

Papa hands us wooden spoons. "¡Cómo te quiero!" we all sing. "Oh, how I love you!" We twirl around and around in a circle of family.

Finally, the kitchen dance slows.
Our song grows sleepy.
Mama sways, feet whispering.
Her hand rubs my back.

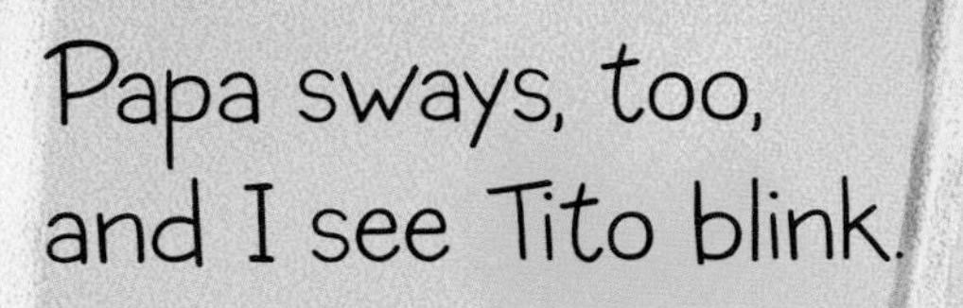

Papa sways, too,
and I see Tito blink.

The whole house is quiet
but for Papa's softest
voice. "Cómo te quiero..."

"Good night—again," Papa tells us.

"Besitos, mi'ja," Mama says,
and she kisses me twice.
"Sweet dreams."

Umm, hmm.